THE VERY COLORFUL CATERPILLAR

BY ANDY SILVERS

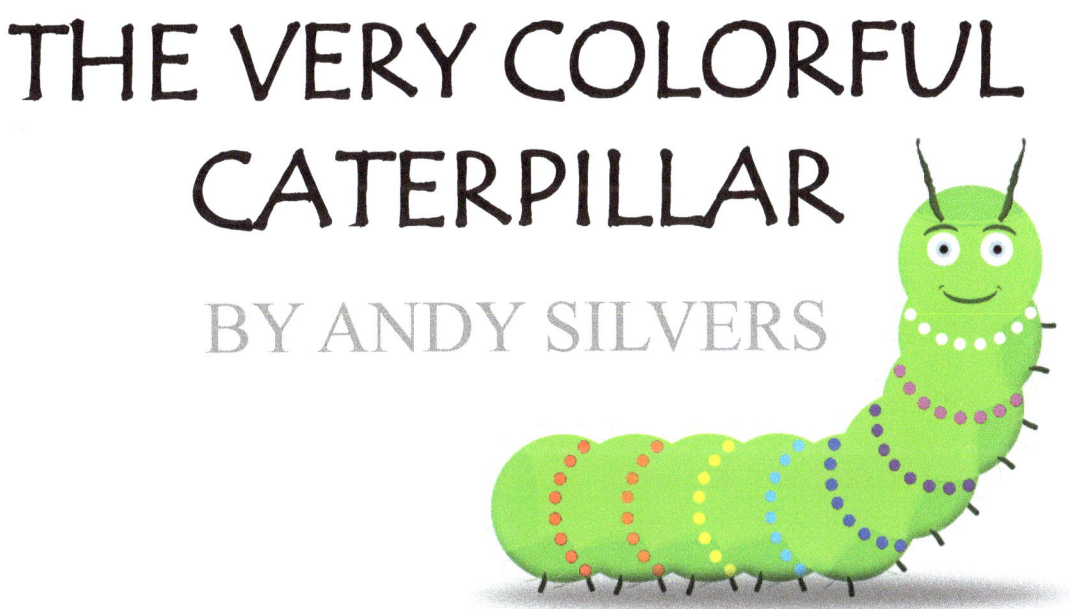

For Margot, the wonderful daughter
of Grayson and Abby Marshall

THE VERY COLORFUL CATERPILLAR

Copyright © 2021 by Andrew Silvers
Published using LULU. *Hendersonville, NC.*
For Margot Marshall.

All rights reserved. No part of this book may be reproduced, sold, or otherwise copied electronically or otherwise without express written permission by the author. The characters and plot are entirely a product of the author's imagination. All images including the cover photo are owned by the author and may not be copied or reproduced for any reason.

Check out <u>Red Sprites and Blue Jets</u> on Amazon. It's a coming-of-age novel for ages 8-12.

Written by Andy Silvers.
Illustrated by Andy Silvers.
https://andysilvers.com/

ISBN (hardcover): 978-1-0879-8334-9
ISBN (paperback): 978-1-300-44629-3

1 70 11 42 88 26 53 77 21 76

A tiny egg sits under a sticky spider's web.

A very colorful caterpillar named Ermine sees the world for the first time.

Beautiful butterflies fly above the small caterpillar.

They flap their wings to fly through the air. Ermine wishes to be colorful like them.

"Hello," says a pretty blue butterfly. "You are VERY colorful. What kind of butterfly will you be?"

"I don't know," Ermine says. "I only know that I am VERY hungry."

The blue butterfly shows Ermine where to find some tasty food.

Maybe Ermine will become
blue like a blueberry.

Or maybe he will be red like a strawberry.

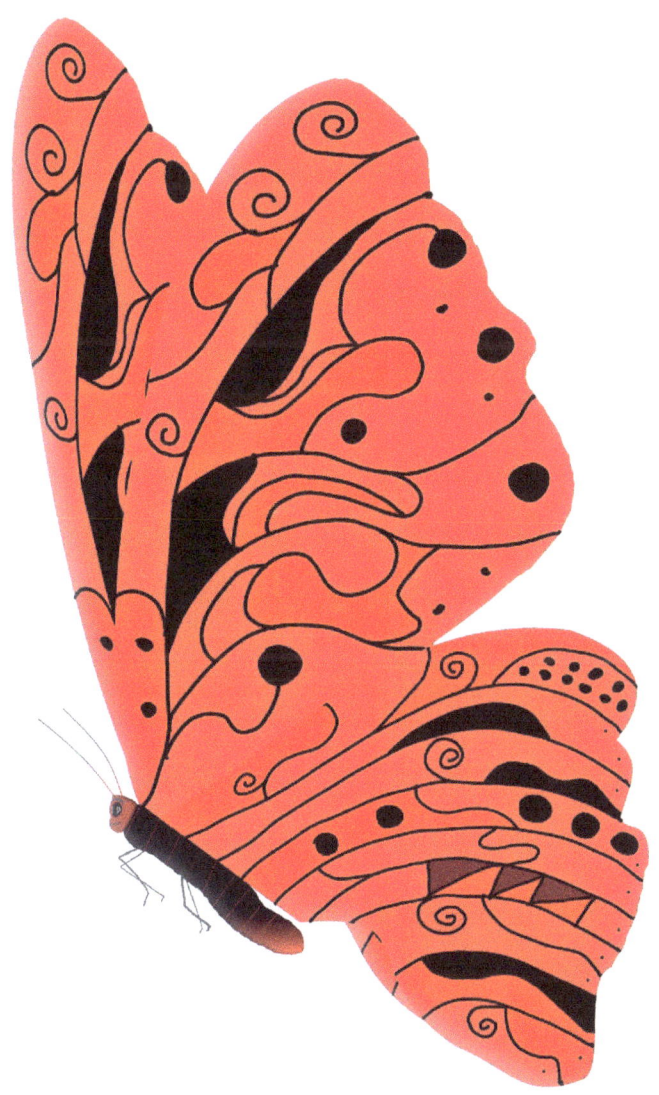
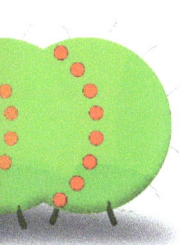

Perhaps he will be green like a Granny Smith apple.

Eating all day makes Ermine VERY tired. He finds a nice white dandelion to sleep on for the night.

While he sleeps, he dreams about what color he will be when he is ready to become a beautiful butterfly.

For a whole week, Ermine eats his way through many tasty snacks.

Maybe he will be yellow like a banana or orange like a peach.

Some butterflies look like a RAINBOW of colors. Maybe Ermine will be as colorful as a birthday cupcake.

Maybe he will have three colors like his friend the Monarch butterfly.

The next day, he makes himself a cocoon to sleep in. He must stay inside his cocoon for ten days.

Finally, he eats his way out of his cocoon. But WAIT! He isn't colorful at all. Little Ermine is totally white!

Ermine isn't a butterfly at all. He's a MOTH. Here come the other moths to say HELLO.

"Hello," they say. "Let's go, Ermine. Life as a moth can be pretty cool too."

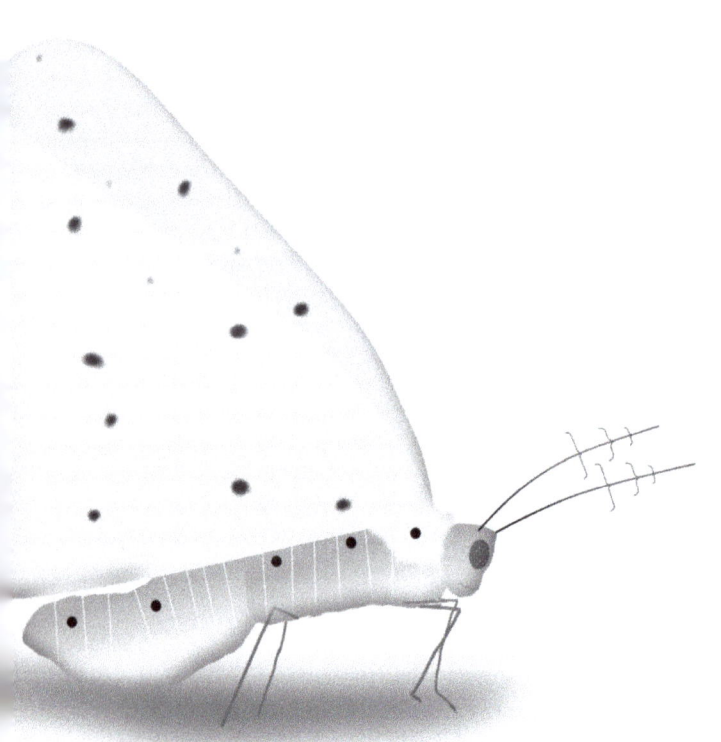

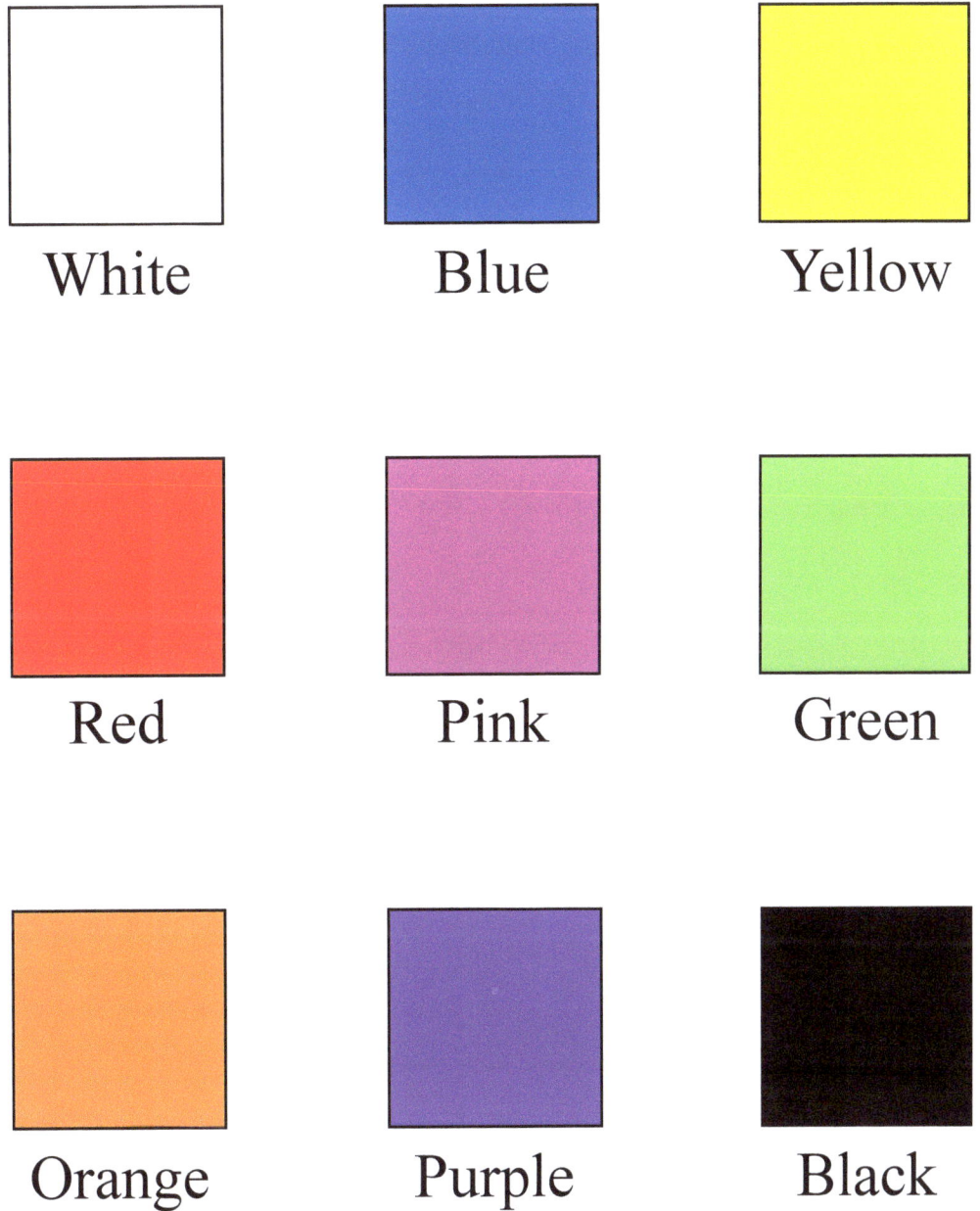

Printed in the USA
CPSIA information can be obtained
at www.ICGtesting.com
LVHW061154181223
766713LV00012B/227